Moonlight Travellers

Moonlight Travellers

Quentin Blake

with Will Self

With 46 illustrations

Thames & Hudson

Quentin Blake is an internationally celebrated illustrator, known for his collaborations with authors such as Roald Dahl, Russell Hoban, John Yeoman, David Walliams and Joan Aiken. A winner of the Kate Greenaway Medal and the Hans Christian Andersen Award, he received a knighthood in 2013 and was made a Chevalier de la Légion d'honneur in 2014. At Thames & Hudson he is series consultant for The Illustrators and in 2019 published his illustrated edition of John Ruskin's *King of the Golden River*.

Will Self is a renowned journalist and literary author. He has written eleven novels and numerous shorter works of fiction and regularly contributes to the *Guardian*, the *New Statesman*, the *New York Times* and the *London Review of Books*. His fiction has been awarded the Geoffrey Faber Memorial Prize and the Aga Khan Prize and shortlisted for the Man Booker Prize.

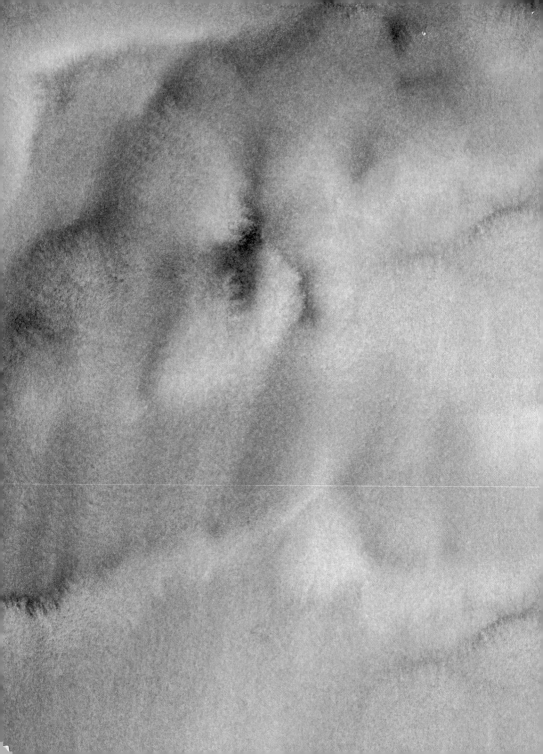

Preface

In 2017 Liz Gilmore, the director of the Jerwood Gallery in Hastings, invited me to put on a show of about a hundred new drawings created especially for the occasion. I chose the title *The Only Way to Travel* as it allowed me to invent a range of fantasy vehicles and creatures to travel on and in.

That many of the pictures would become so sombre was something that I had not envisaged, but when the show opened, among them were a series of twenty such pictures: *The Moonlight Travellers*. They were vertical (portrait) in format, and later I produced twenty more of the same drawings but in a horizontal format. Those are the pictures in this book. They are drawn on sheets of Arches fin watercolour paper with a reed pen, and Payne's Grey watercolour. Only the colour of the moon varies from picture to picture.

Quentin Blake

Will Self

1

You're riding on the very tip-top of wind-tossed boughs – or standing in the crow's nest of an ocean-going sailing ship. You sense this through the shifting currents of sleep, as they carry you, sliding over somnolent boils and into gentle eddies; sense this as a parent lofts you from the back of a car, or a pushchair, before bearing you safely to bed. Is there ever anything sweeter than this, the enfolding arms that are both impersonal and unimpeachably intimate? And then the descent, in a fall that's at once free and utterly secure – a fall that ends happily ... drowsily ... in the fast-warming safety-swaddle of the covers. You lift your face for a last look at the world, and there, scudding behind a cloudy tracery, you see her, the goddess Selene, staring down at you with serenely loving indifference.

Over the years, every night-time journey you've taken has, in some way, conformed to this piercingly nostalgic paradigm: cars, buses, trains, boats and aeroplanes – all, at some point in the transit, would seem to be moving with the steady gait of a careful parent. But then, at other times, it felt as if all that supported you was some strange contraption. Perhaps you were like me as a child, trying to build go-carts out of old pram wheels, or to cobble together from hangers and black plastic bags kites capable of lifting you aloft, or to blast off for the moon in cardboard-tube rockets fuelled by 3-IN-ONE Oil. It was when I imagined myself balanced upon – or dangling below – such vehicles that I rumbled and swooped and shot precipitately, my parabola kissing the tips of those wind-tossed boughs. Did you, I wonder, kiss them with me?

At night the traveller is thrown on his mettle – there can be no dereliction of the duty to maintain course through the darkness, darkness that is not absence of light, but has the semi-solid character of de Selby's 'black air'. If you've started before sunset, then you'll have seen the light leached from the sky – yet it isn't until the moon rises that you realize the colours all went with it as well. For what lies before you now is a black-and-white world, near-infinitely gradated, and with the sparks and scintillations of silver leaf applied to real ones. This realm, so complex, so delicately wrought, bears little resemblance to the world of the day; to journey by day is to make prosaic progress straight from A to B, but the moonlight traveller flits from L to O, to V and E – so constructing, foot by foot, his own metrical poetry.

I sense another walking with us – a third figure, ghostly and flitting, whose round spectacles shine brightly in the darkness. But when I confront him, he melts away into mustiness ... the cloth wound round the handles of old tennis racquets ... the aroma of gutta-percha ... and esters of sweat. Don't you see him? Don't you? If I address you thus – insistently, persistently – doesn't that somehow make of you a part of me? For we're confined together in this text, you and I, swaddled in its warm words the way our parents wrapped us in blankets when we were children. And what is life in the final analysis? The unnamed poet descants of a chief's hall crowded with his feasting retainers; of mead drunk, songs sung and all the happy fellowship to be found there. And what of the little bird that flies into the hall? What does she feel, as she flaps over the upturned faces to the accompaniment of tumultuous laughter: that this is her real life, while what preceded it is all darkness – a darkness into which, all too soon, she'll flit?

It's the same for us, surely – with this important difference: our real life takes place in these all too brief moonlit flits, as we escape both the day's banalities and flee the dubieties of darkness. We are crepuscular creatures to a fault, hiding in the gloom that affords us the luxury of our scepticism. Who are we? We are legions of lunar voyagers, existing for mere moments of ardency in this argent light – and so we drowse, we rouse, and we sleep again; each relapse carrying us further back and further down, until we awake finally to find ourselves borne once more by those encircling arms.

I once saw the Queen's Guide to the Sands: he was on his stilts, moving with a heron's stiff-legged and head-dipping gait over slick sable surfaces, at once unzipping his image from a steely sky and affixing it to this most debatable of lands, where waters came rushing in, dissolving distance, time and everything solid. On he came, and there were prayer flags fluttering in his eyes, for he had seen the jewel in the heart of the lotus, and he had seen the moon come up over the shoulders of the fells to the north, and he had felt the clouds boil and stream in his own cold-cockled heart, for he could never erase the memory of the van sinking beneath the silty waves. I think I saw you there, with him – he took you by the hand and you went willingly with him, away into the far west, with the cockle-pickers, to Tír na nÓg.

I remember this: going for a night walk with you cradled in my arms. I recall this: you going for a night walk with me cradled in your arms. I remember us pacing between low and prickly bushes, careful lest we scratch our bare ankles. I remember the heady aromas released by the darkness and the slight dampness of the slow-falling dew: clean, green grassiness – and a bouquet of herbs that suggested we were somewhere southern and Mediterranean. And I looked down at your dear face, gilded by the moonlight – and I looked up at your dear face, averted from the moonlight. And we told each other about our moon powers: the ability we both have to squint at the moon in such a way that long and lemony moonbeams thrust out from its cratered face and then with-draw. Funny, isn't it – we both thought that we were the only person in the world who possessed this amazing ability to let there be light – and now we realize that no, everyone else is godlike as well.

So, we stood on a smooth eminence, looking out over a wide and shallow valley, massy with the doubly silvered canopies of olive trees; here and there the occasional quill of a cypress dipping itself into the inky darkness. A dog howled in the mid-distance, where the whitened and marmoreal bones of ruined temples and tumbledown follies gleamed from between the trees. Over it all lay a thin and gauzy curtain of mist, which seemed to ripple and curl in the moonlight. Oh, the moon! Oh, Selene, you goddess – so serenely indifferent as you push and pull at us, dragging our humours about in our wine-sack bodies! It occurred to us – you and I – that the only appropriate thing to do, besides bathe in this serious moonlight, was to worship her.

2

Swaying back and forth on the animal's broad back, feeling its surly gravity shift beneath your own – this would be unstable enough, but then the beast lows pitifully, before homing in and rubbing its scabrous flank against the softly abrasive weave, a motion that precipitates you, giggling, on to the sofa. You knew then a truth you've long since forgotten: that just as you yourself have moon powers, so the moon has power over you – power of your wine-sack body with its wine-dark contents that slosh back and forth, pulled hither and thither by its surly gravity. Yes, Selene has power over you: the power to confer imagination, or to withdraw it; to let new visions flood into your psyche, or to drain them out of you in a tide that will ebb ... forever.

The sweet-smelling confection of straw and dung snakes inside your sleepy nostrils, and you realize you're standing beside a rough and lime-washed wall. Unexpected little zephyrs stroke your face, and you have a sense that somewhere there's a softly heaving sea puckering where it's stroked by the rays of a coolly cruising wintry moon. Then ... well, there's nothing ever quite like this, is there: the moment when, your foot in the stirrup, you commit to the metamorphosis – for this is no mere pivoting: the point where you tip from two legs to four, but the initiation, time after time, of a holy symbiosis, as human becomes centaur. And off you go, clattering across the stable-yard, then clopping over the sands. You sway, feeling the ornate caparison slip between your thighs and the haunches of the beast that bears you – you are the moonlight traveller whose horse crops the forest's ferny floor, but you're also the horse who lowers its head, refusing the jerk of its reins.

The moon drives everyone mad – you know that, well enough. But this is no lycanthropic or otherwise spooky metamorphosis: it's far stranger than that. You rise from your bed and, leaving your nightclothes lying coiled and cooling on the floor, you flee out the back door into the garden. The moonlight has electroplated the frivolous flowers, and so they range along their narrow beds, sentinel and sinisterly beautiful. You stand, confused by such clarity: is this night-time at all, or a scene being shot in full daylight, in such a way that all concerned – actors, directors, producers, designers and audience – can readily suspend disbelief?

Because here they come, marching towards you across the field at the far end of the garden, and you rush to join them, your bare ankles and shins scratched by the stubble and bitten by the bugs that whirl up into the air. They carry torches with them, their beams fingering the darkness – and at your rendezvous, they ease these upright into the soil between the roots of a sentinel bush, so that they form a single shining beacon. Over this scintillating bush they throw a sheet – such that the great globe seems to have been drawn down into a cloudy chamber, over the eerily glowing billows of which worm the bamboozled muons and positrons, their antennae twitching, their tattered wings fluttering.

Is there any greater pathos to be had than this: the fates of small creatures, driven on by instincts that admit no intercession by God or reason? Yes, there is: the fates of small creatures driven on to the super-heated surfaces of fraudulent bulbs – those decoys of the moon. 'Is there anyone there?' You cried up to the shuttered window, and when no one opened it, you yanked at the bridle, pulled again, until at last the horse's head rose up and the two of you undulated on along the path between the trees. A canny soul, you comforted yourself with this expertise: knowing the hour of its rising and its setting, if you kept the waxing moon on your right shoulder, you could be certain of finding your way, so kept on, as the path fell down into deep ravines and then switchbacked its way up again. Poor moths – poor bamboozled things. And yes: there are indeed bats with baby faces scudding through the violet light; and yes, there are sounds high in the air, the murmurs of maternal lamentation. But who is the fourth who crawls beside you, head down against the blackened wall of the night sky? Is it perhaps your moth-self, the part of you that repeats these same cosmic mistakes again and again, forever expecting a different result?

It isn't a broad-backed beast that bore you – and that's no silvered sea, but a swamp bilious with blue-green algae, out of which the wire-mesh of discarded shopping trolleys glows with a worrying lambency. In the faint moonlight, the grass is moaning – there's a flash of lightning, then a damp gust of wind; you sense the clamminess of the coming dawn. And now you see that you've been as foolish as any Lepidoptera, and as blinkered as any horse, for all you've done is to keep the bush with the torches espaliered to its roots on your right shoulder, as you've ridden around it, again and again. While the shadows have lengthened ... and lengthened some more, stretching out to enfold you in the tremulousness of a never-ending moment.

3

There's nothing more prosaic – at least, at this end of human history – than a car journey. How very few of our remote ancestors left their African homeland, and headed through the Middle East to Asia and Europe – a mere car-load, one might say. Theirs was an epochal progress: slow, tentative, encountering at each centenarian step things never known theretofore by humans. They took with them their tool assemblages, arrived at patiently by tens of thousands of trials and errors. Bone fishhooks, stone hand axes, fire-hardened wooden spears, woven nets – all fabricated from natural materials, technologies that seemed more akin to the bowers of the eponymous birds, or beavers' dams.

In France, the fin-de-siècle style dubbed Art Nouveau was, in reality, the last gasp of the old vegetal and organic forms – the final spluttering of Dylan Thomas's quick green fuse as it was turned not to stone, but iron. Annealed into the ornate coping of the Metro stations designed by Hector Guimard are the stems of flowers that have remained thrusting motion-lessly for decades. The same sinuous lines and pleasingly ovoid shapes are to be found in the Citroën Deux Chevaux, the humble workhorse of French agriculture – and of motor transport generally – well into the second half of the twentieth century. And, of course, cars acquire tool assemblages of their own, which consist not just of the obvious wrench-and-jack combination in the boot, but also discoid tins of boiled sweets, chamois leathers stuffed into glove compartments, and

St Christopher medallions on lengths of silver chain dangling from the rear-view mirror. Every car I've ever owned has possessed a unique tool assemblage – and I'm quite sure the same is true of yours.

Leaving a sleepy village hidden behind a long line of dunes on the east coast, I think of the German Ocean, which lies gunboat-heavy and gunmetal-gleaming beneath the cold rays of a winter moon. I've been sitting all evening on a narrow settle beside an open fire in the cosy snug of an ancient pub, listening to the thwock! and grumble of bar billiards players as I sup, one after another, pints of the local ale, which goes by the name of Broadside. North of here, on another moonlit night three centuries ago, the English and the Dutch fleets had at one another with ball and canister shot; to the south, half a millennium still earlier, a prosperous city of churches and well-founded merchants' houses, on a stormy night when the moon raced along behind a ragged jalousie of cloud, shrugged, groaned and, turning over, slid beneath the relentless swell. Even by day, this is a debatable land – a melange of dank marsh and parched moor – and under moonlight its several planes slide into and out of each other, fold over and under, as the little car grumbles to the end of the metalled roadway.

You've been sitting beside me in silence all evening, knowing better than to remark upon the cosmic solecism of a driver powered by ethyl alcohol – and you say nothing when I unclip the canvas roof, and open it out so that the interior of the car is filled with liquid moonlight. The great Polynesian navigators, who plied the Pacific in their reed-woven boats, thought of themselves not as moving between A and B, but as fixed points around which the cosmos of stars, planets, moon and islands revolved. You can appreciate how this allowed them to attune themselves to a vast amount of sensory and perceptual data – from the wind on their upturned faces, to the flotsam borne on the ocean currents, and the angles at which moonbeams subtend – all of which is lost to us in our own era of angular geometry.

Dowsing the lights, I explain to you that there are green lanes and ancient holloways connecting the coastal village to the isolated dell, miles away in the hinterland, where my cottage lies. We have no need of our own illumination, when the goddess Selene rises above the skeletal boughs, altogether indifferent to their scratches. To drive under such conditions – the car's engine racing as we dip and flip along the rutted track – is to set sail on an earthsea, out of which rear the rocky headlands formed by ancient tree stumps. And as we progress, crunching through fast-frosting puddles, I regale you with tales of other moonlit drives: those nights when I set off from the city, full of youth and amphetamine, to plunge end over end, down the time-tunnels carved from the black air by my headlights.

These epochal car rides would take me from the city of my birth, to either the far north or the further south. On stopping to jettison or take on ballast, I'd find that the moon – which had kept faith with me, skipping from chimney to pylon to treetop – had halted as well, and so we'd stand staring at each other. What beings, I'd wonder, might inhabit this vast and satellite cheese, which, with its vermiculated crust and orange-umber hue, so recalled – to my mind at least – the Boule de Lille, mandated by Louis XIV? When we resumed our journey, it seemed to me that they'd joined us – these adventurous Selenians – and now disported themselves on the back seat, sucking boiled sweets and querying, quite reasonably, if we were there yet.

4

I joined the train late – and it was quite a difficult matter simply getting my vehicle on board. It's a delicately constructed flying machine, you see, with the long, transparent and beautifully traced wings of a damsel fly. The hand-crank for lowering the wings worked fine, but the smaller one, which pulls them together in a complex three-dimensional concertina, jammed, and I had to have stiff words with an employee of the railway, who tried to force it, nearly tearing one. The thought of arriving in the middle of the night, and finding myself unable to take flight, didn't bear thinking about.

The train itself was made up from several different kinds of rolling stock: old British Rail carriages, in their dark and pale blue livery; little cars from the funicular up to Sacre Coeur; a wide-gauge behemoth of a coach from the Trans-Siberian express; and, at the front, bearing the arms of the Grand Trunk Railway, a huge old continental-class steam engine, which sat grunting and belching out steamy puffballs. Once aboard, I made my way from compartment to compartment, in search of my own couchette. Live chickens hung by their feet from hooks implanted in the quilted silk ceiling coverings; a trad' jazz band was warming up in the caboose, and the parps and poots of their brass instruments seemed to anticipate our future velocity.

On the floors and windowsills; in the toilets, the luggage racks and the vaporous galley; everywhere, in short, where there was any free space, it was occupied by one or other of the Milenian men. They were small and swarthy, dressed in beige worsted trousers and jerkins that were tightly lashed to all four of their stubby limbs and thickset trunks by cross-threaded leather thongs. The Milenian men brewed up red tea on tiny portable clay stoves fuelled with pungent buffalo chips, then worked at their carving, seemingly oblivious to the smoke and unable to hear the persistent whine of the mosquitoes. As for their tall and elegant womenfolk, with their down-curving scimitar noses and high mantillas, they disported themselves on the Moroccan leather and worn moquette seats; the very picture of refinement as they ate honey cakes, then smeared the sticky residue on their necks, their cheeks and the Brilliantine-stained antimacassars.

Eventually I found it: a small, tubular sleeping berth that thrust out from the wall of the carriage to form an odd sort of observation car – for the thick material from which it was made was altogether transparent. Sitting in there, reading, was a heavyset and heavily bearded man in his sixties, who, as I climbed up the little ladder and squirmed inside, put his book aside. It was an old Baedeker. 'Have you ever,' he remarked edgily, 'been trapped in a confined space for a night with an extremely violent man?' I replied that I wasn't aware of this having happened to me, but you can never be sure, since all sorts of bizarre things may – and, indeed, often do – happen while you sleep. The man – who told me his name was Grenville – then asked further: 'Would you like to hear my tale of what it was like when I was confined in such a manner?'

I mounted the short ladder, and worked my way inside the sleeping compartment as an infantryman does under fire, my elbows playing the part of vestigial legs. I laid my head in the crook of Grenville's arm, and smelt the revenants of a thousand past pipes tickling up my nostrils, together with tussocks of his beard. 'Then I'll begin,' he waffled. 'I had joined the train late – there had been such a business getting my vehicle on board. It's a delicately constructed flying machine, you see, with the long, transparent and beautifully traced wings of a damsel fly. The hand-crank for lowering the wings worked fine, but the smaller one, which pulls them together in a complex three-dimensional concertina, jammed, and I had to have stiff words with an employee of the railway, who tried to force it, nearly breaking one. The thought of arriving in the middle of the night, and being unable to take flight, didn't bear thinking about ... '

He bumbled on as, with a heavy shrug, the train started off. The Milenian men began to sing in their own language: wistful words that wafted away in the slipstream. The train gathered pace, and as it reached the long, curving viaduct that carries the tracks out of the city, its wheels' paradiddle incorporated cymbal sounds and rimshots. Through the viaduct's lattice of rusty girders I saw the moon – but she evaded me by plunging into the river, and the last thing I remember, as I was lulled into sleep, was the sight of her blanched face, staring up at me from beneath the gelid waters.

5

The rust was the colour of water; the water was the colour of rust. The coffee was also the colour of rust, and it cost a single rust-coloured drachma. When the cup had been drained there was a small crescent-shape of rusty sediment at the bottom. The clanking and rattling of the anchor chain being raised strongly implied that a counter-weight had been chucked overboard, and even though there was only this evidence, I nevertheless felt it was me who'd been pitched unceremoniously into the wine-dark Aegean. Oh, and you were there as well, wrapped up with me in an awkward embrace. Down we went, sliding from one cold fathom to the next colder one. Looking up we saw this: the two spiralling trails of silvery bubbles twining around each other to form the genome of our watery dissolution – while, above this, the moon lay face down in the sea.

Clambering back up the ladder and flopping over the taffrail, I saw a headline on a limp sheet of newsprint that lay in a pool of rusty water: 'THE KING IS DEAD,' it read in Greek – a language of which, up until that precise moment, I'd had no comprehension whatsoever. You saw it, too – understood it as well – so, from then on, if you recall, we agreed to keep each other awake with pinches and light slaps, because that was all we knew: that a king was dead, but not which one, and, fearing it might be the heavenly one, we determined to keep our eyes on the sidereal array, willing it to stay up in the empyrean, until the dawn chorus went up: 'Long live the King!'

Actually, it didn't matter, did it? Neither of us could sleep after that chilly immersion, followed by such dreadful news

– and, frankly, we were both amazed that our fellow passengers could find repose on those steely decks, which vibrated beneath their supine bodies as the engines hammered away in the bowels of the vessel. No, neither of us could sleep – so we drank little plastic cup upon cup of the oxidized coffee and talked all about everything, the way people do when they passionately want to get to know one another, and lean into each other, seeking to discern the shape of an idea before it's fully formed, so as to catch hold of it and haul it, kicking, into the aquamarine atmosphere of that midnight saloon. From time to time we'd promenade on the deck, arm in arm, watching the endless fractal patterning of the sea, as it grew older and then younger beneath the waning moon.

Which, by the time we'd sailed through the rock-ragged passage and entered the vast and flooded caldera, hung hornéd in a sky, which, as it became paler, was infused with pinks, blues and mauves – all so freshly mixed that it seemed to us as if this was their very first unveiling. The other passengers took their time disembarking; looking back at the ship from halfway up the precipitate path to the top, I saw them still combing out their pigtails, shouldering their sleeping rolls and strapping to their broad backs their even broader – and double-headed – battleaxes. Up ahead of us, the houses built on the very lip of the caldera snagged jaggedly against the dawn sky – and when we looked back down again, the ship that had borne us there had already cast off, and was sink-sailing rapidly into the wine-dark waters, with brilliant bubble-chains trailing from its rapidly disappearing stern.

Whitewashed houses spread smoothly along the curving horns of the caldera's rim, and shone in the morning moon-light. But many were derelict, and as we neared them we could sense their emptiness: nerveless teeth, implanted in ancient gums. We unrolled our own bedding at last and lay down to rest. A tractor beam filled with vaporous swirls lanced down from the clouds above, grabbed hold, pulled me up a half mile or so, then flipped me over so I could see the hornéd island floating in the ever-mutating and sunless sea. And I saw you there, way down below me, sleeping on the whitewashed roof of the abandoned house and dreaming your dreams of flight.

6

... in the middle of the night – which was a pretty small place, given we were travelling so very fast – you woke, and I regretted the Dubonnet miniatures I'd stolen from the dimpled-steel bins in the galley. They'd pushed me down into the cold hold of myself for a couple of hours – but here I was, coming up for rebreathed air. While there you were, gulping like a fish, or a whited sepulchre, or the gibbous moon in a hot south London sky. Then, as I opened the little circular plastic shutter, and squinted out through the two layers of thick transparent plastic, I vouchsafed (if you recall) my envy – yes, envy – for the quasi-homonymics, *hiboux* and *hublot*. That took us back, didn't it? Back and back and back to the semi-submerged wheat fields, and the moon taking off fast over the Essex flatlands, by this power alone, sending out a silk ripple across the estuary. On that occasion, at least, we'd resisted the impulse to ride hard. So what if we could've still made it into Southend in time for a standing fish supper. So we stood instead, savouring those moments, then mounted our penny farthings and bowled along the road, all our flags fluttering, the barn owls flying alongside in shifting formations, their fuzzy wings so acoustically null that with each down stroke they absorbed the death rattles of the roosting crows and the putter of a distant tractor, still at it ploughing gulls into the heavy till …

… the moon hangs in the same sky we fly through – or possibly one adjacent. Tonight of all nights, she has a face – a beautiful human face, obscured by a cratered mask. This is the moon Méliès's astronauts set off for, in their painful bullet of a ship .... This is the cheesy one, beloved of children and animators – and, as the jets whisper us through the stratosphere, we stare upon its beloved visage .... Surely this is the primordial form of love itself: at once achingly familiar – and completely inconnu .... What can she be thinking? As Yuri Gagarin transitions to Valentina Tereshkova ... the Moon draws us into her, rendering us all female in such heavy swell .... That was the point of it, surely, the epitome of those phallic craft ... designed by ex-Nazis, flown by men with the Right Stuff ... they embarked on the most subversive journey ever, its manifest destination quite different from their latent intent – which was what? Perhaps they felt that by responding to these immemorial ebbs and flows they would somehow reconnect to the primordial ocean ... by landing in this barren and arid place they would re-green their poisoned world .... We're in agreement, aren't we, you and I? Tonight is our night – the fulfilment of our dreams. And how can mere sublunary terror match up to the sublime immensity of space? No doubt our fellow passengers will be a little upset when the pilot announces our new destination – but then they'll have a while to get used to it .... Days, then months, raiding the dimpled-steel bins until all the Dubonnet miniatures (and everything else) are gone.

How will it feel when, at long last, we can speak – quite casually – of earthrise and earthset ...? When this silent big sibling of ours, marbled blue and green, rolls around so majestically in our sky? It will feel as it did when we awoke, feeling the swaddling covers slip softly away and the cool of the night smarm against our flanks – then landed, softly and yet more securely, in the enfolding arms of the third who walks beside us.

Quentin Blake

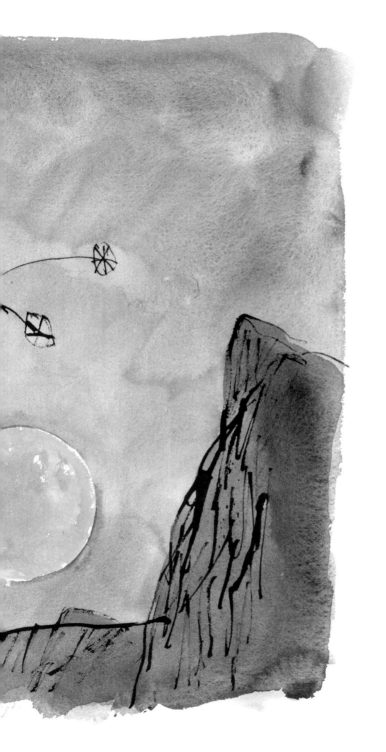

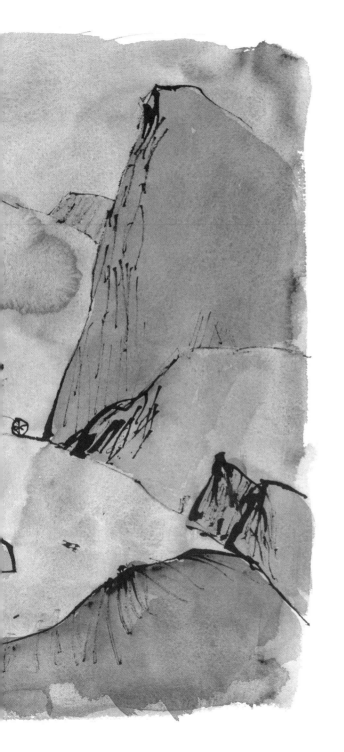

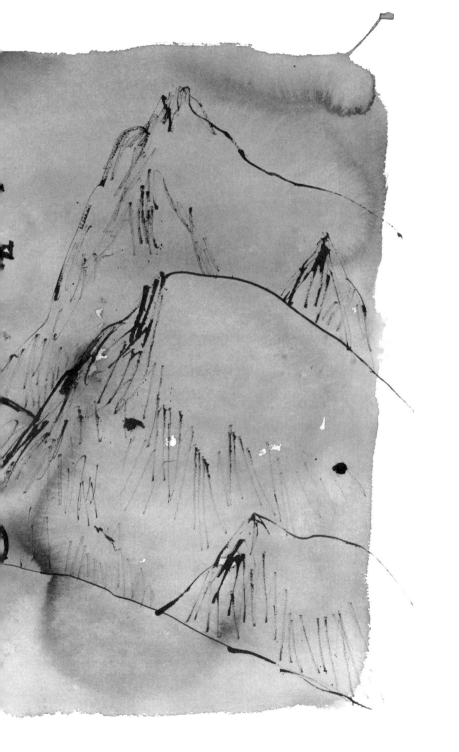

Editor's Note

It is a special occasion when a major visual artist and a major literary artist can make a book together. So it is a particular pleasure to launch into the world this unique collaboration between two creative minds at the height of their powers, whose work is often seen in very different spheres. Quentin Blake has created a remarkable series of drawings with unmatched artistic skill, insight and intrigue, and Will Self, in responding to them, affords the reader the pleasure of exploring the creative turns, of memory or fantasy, that take us on a very special journey. The theme of light and dark that touches both the written and the visual throughout this book of moonlit journeys resonates across the boundaries that too often dominate our lives and thought. I hope that the creative inspiration that lies at its heart will in turn reach beyond the page to accompany your own travels and encounters.

Roger Thorp

First published in the United States of America in 2019 by Thames & Hudson Inc., 500 Fifth Avenue, New York, New York, 10110

www.thamesandhudsonusa.com

Library of Congress Control Number 2019932286

ISBN 978-0-500-02273-3

Printed in China by RR Donnelley